A NOTE TO PARENTS

When your children are ready to "step into reading," giving them the right books is as crucial as giving them the right food to eat. **Step into Reading Books** and STAR WARS® **JEDI READERS** present exciting stories and information reinforced with lively, colorful illustrations that make learning to read fun, satisfying, and worthwhile. They are priced so that acquiring an entire library of them is affordable. And they are beginning readers with a difference—they're written on five levels.

Early Step into Reading Books are designed for brand-new readers, with large type and only one or two lines of very simple text per page. **Step 1 Books** feature the same easy-to-read type as the Early Step into Reading Books, but with more words per page. **Step 2 Books** are both longer and slightly more difficult, while **Step 3 Books** introduce readers to paragraphs and fully developed plot lines. **Step 4 Books** offer exciting fiction and nonfiction for the increasingly independent reader.

The grade levels assigned to the five steps—preschool through kindergarten for the Early Books, preschool through grade 1 for Step 1, grades 1 through 3 for Step 2, grades 2 through 3 for Step 3, and grades 2 through 4 for Step 4—are intended only as guides. Some children move through all five steps very rapidly; others climb the steps over a period of several years. Either way, these books will help your child "step into reading" in style!

www.randomhouse.com/kids
www.starwars.com

Library of Congress Cataloging-in-Publication Data
Thomas, Jim K., 1970–
Dangers of the core / by Jim Thomas ; illustrated by Boris Vallejo.
p.   cm. — (Jedi readers. A step 3 book)
SUMMARY: Jar Jar Binks and two Jedi Knights journey through the dangerous core of the planet Naboo.
ISBN 0-375-80002-6 (trade). — ISBN 0-375-90002-0 (lib. bdg.)
[1. Science fiction.]   I. Vallejo, Boris, ill.   II. Title.   III. Series: Jedi readers. Step 3 book.   PZ7.T366956Dan   1999   [Fic]—dc21   98-48535

Printed in the United States of America   10 9 8 7 6 5 4 3 2 1
STEP INTO READING is a registered trademark of Random House, Inc.

JEDI READERS

STAR WARS®

EPISODE I

DANGERS of the CORE

A Step 3 Book

by Jim Thomas

illustrated by Boris Vallejo

Random House
New York

1
The Swamp

Qui-Gon Jinn was running as fast as he could. A powerful engine roared right behind him. The Trade Federation transport was getting closer. *Too close!* he thought.

The transport carried an army of deadly battle droids. The planet Naboo was being invaded. Qui-Gon had to get to the city of Theed and warn the Queen!

All around him, animals were running for cover—except one.

A tall, froglike creature sat in the mud right in the Jedi Knight's path. It was eating a clam with its long, sticky tongue.

"Watch out!" Qui-Gon yelled.

The creature looked up and saw Qui-Gon. Then it saw the huge transport behind him. Its eyes grew wide.

"Oh, nooo!" it cried, grabbing the Jedi's robes. "Hep me, hep me!"

Qui-Gon looked back. The transport was almost on top of them!

Qui-Gon pushed the creature down into the muddy water and dove in after it.

The transport roared overhead.

Qui-Gon sat up and watched the transport disappear into the mist. The creature jumped up and gave Qui-Gon a big hug.

"Oyi! I luv yous!" it cried. "Meesa your humble servant."

Qui-Gon smiled. "That won't be necessary," he said.

"Oh, but tis!" the creature insisted. "Yousa saved Jar Jar Binks's life. Tis a life debt I owe."

Suddenly, a man ran out of the mist. It was Qui-Gon's student, Obi-Wan Kenobi. A battle droid on a STAP was chasing him.

Qui-Gon drew his lightsaber. The battle droid fired, but Qui-Gon deflected the blasts right back. The droid was destroyed.

"Thank you, Master," said Obi-Wan. "Naboo is crawling with battle droids. How can we avoid the army and get to Theed?"

"Um…excuse meesa," said Jar Jar. "Meesa knows a way."

Obi-Wan noticed Jar Jar for the first time. "Who is this?" he asked Qui-Gon.

Qui-Gon smiled. "This is my new friend, Jar Jar."

"Meesa home nearby," said Jar Jar. "City called Otoh Gunga. Hidden, tis."

Qui-Gon nodded. "Sounds good. Show us the way, Jar Jar."

Obi-Wan was shocked. "Master," he said, "surely you're not going to listen to this…creature?"

Qui-Gon smiled to himself. Obi-Wan was a good student, but he still had much to learn.

"My young Padawan," Qui-Gon said, "remember: all living things are connected. Even something that *seems* unimportant can affect us in important ways."

Obi-Wan frowned. "Yes, Master."

The roar of the landing transports was getting closer. They had to hurry.

"Weesa goin underwater, okay?" Jar Jar asked.

Qui-Gon nodded. He and Obi-Wan pulled breathing masks from their belts. Jar Jar dove into the water, and the Jedi followed.

2
Otoh Gunga

The Jedi followed Jar Jar deeper and
deeper underwater. Finally, they spied a
strange light. As they got closer, Qui-Gon
and Obi-Wan could see it came from a city
enclosed in huge glowing bubbles.

Getting into Otoh Gunga was easy. Jar Jar swam up to one of the bubbles and pushed right through. The Jedi followed him. They were inside!

The three found themselves in a crowded city square. Right away, someone started shouting at them.

"Uh-oh," Jar Jar said.

Four Gungan guards surrounded them. They rode two-legged animals called kaadu and carried long electropoles.

"What do they want?" Obi-Wan asked Jar Jar.

Jar Jar looked down at his feet. "Um…meesa forget to tell yous. Meesa been banished. Meesa never supposed to come back here!"

The guards led Jar Jar and the two Jedi to a room high in a tower. Several important Gungans sat in a semicircle against one wall. One sat on a platform higher than the rest. His name was Boss Nass.

Boss Nass laughed when he saw Jar Jar. The guards took Jar Jar aside and locked him in chains.

Qui-Gon spoke directly to Boss Nass.

"The planet is being invaded," Qui-Gon said. "We are trying to warn the people on the surface."

Boss Nass snorted. "Weesa no like da Naboo people. Weesa no hep dem."

Obi-Wan stepped forward. "But after the army conquers them, they'll come down here for you."

Boss Nass shook his head. "Meesa no tink so. That army not know about ussen."

"You and the people on the surface are connected," Qui-Gon said quietly. "What happens to them *will* affect you."

Boss Nass snorted again. "Weesa no care."

"Very well," Qui-Gon said. He looked into Boss Nass's eyes and slowly waved his hand. It was a Jedi mind trick.

"You're going to speed us on our way," Qui-Gon said softly.

"Weesa goin to speed yous on yous way," Boss Nass said.

"You're going to give us a transport," said Qui-Gon.

"Weesa goin to give yous a transport," said Boss Nass.

"Thank you," Qui-Gon said with another wave of his hand.

"Thank you," Boss Nass repeated.

The two Jedi turned to leave the room. Qui-Gon paused in front of Jar Jar.

Jar Jar looked sadly at Qui-Gon. "Any hep you can do for me?" he asked.

"We don't have time for this, Master," Obi-Wan said.

Qui-Gon shook his head. His student *still* did not understand.

"But we do, my young Padawan," Qui-Gon said. "Already Jar Jar has helped us. By bringing us here, he helped us escape the droid army. And we now have a transport to get to Theed. Perhaps Jar Jar will help us again."

Qui-Gon walked back to Boss Nass. "I saved Jar Jar's life," Qui-Gon said. "He owes me a life debt."

The Boss looked at Jar Jar. "Is this true, Binks?"

Jar Jar nodded.

"Very well," Boss Nass said. "Hissen life belongs to yous, outlander. Guards will lead yous to a transport. Da speedest way to Theed is goin through da planet core."

Qui-Gon bowed. The guards released Jar Jar. The threesome was free to go.

"Oh, no! Da core tis berry bad. I all-must rather die here!" moaned Jar Jar.

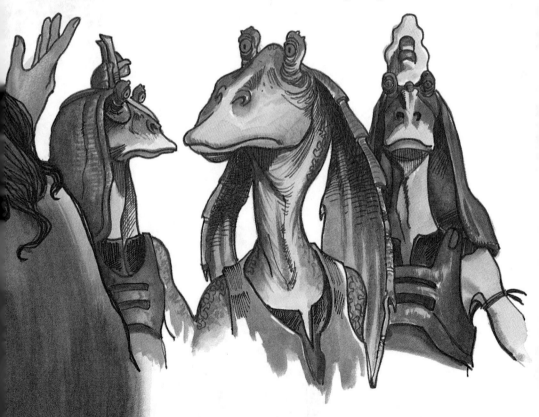

3
The Core

As promised, Boss Nass gave Jar Jar and the Jedi a small submarine called a bongo. Obi-Wan piloted the bongo, with Jar Jar beside him as navigator.

Jar Jar shook in his seat.

"Da core sure is bad bombin dangerous!" he said.

"That's okay, Jar Jar," Qui-Gon said. "The Force will guide us. We have to take the fastest way."

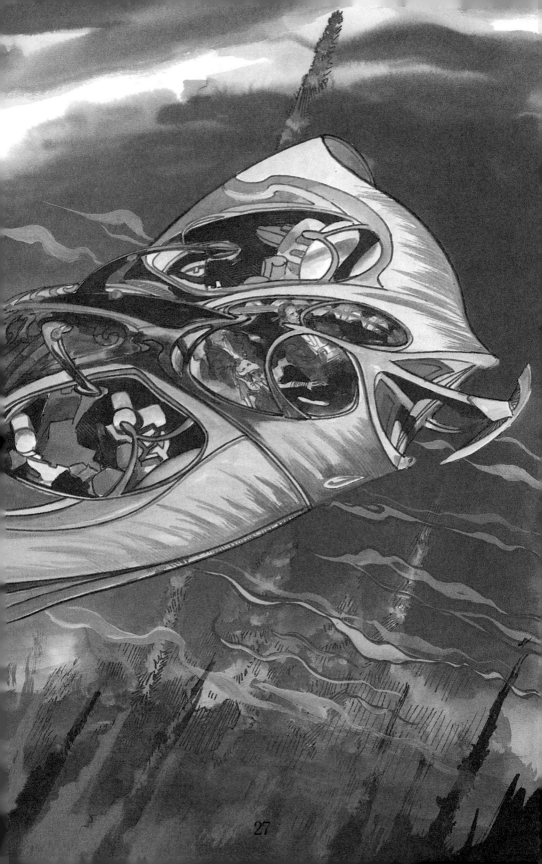

As Obi-Wan drove the bongo into
deeper water, the light from the city
began to fade.

He switched on the bongo's headlights.
In the beautiful coral reefs ahead were
many tunnels leading deeper into the core.

Obi-Wan fiddled with the controls and
headed into one of the tunnels.

Suddenly, the bongo jerked. Then it started going backward!

"Uh-oh," Jar Jar said, looking back into the murky water. "Opee sea killer!"

The huge fish had snared the bongo with its long, gooey tongue. It was pulling them into its mouth!

"Full speed ahead," Qui-Gon said.

Obi-Wan hit the throttle, and the bongo shot backward—right into the sea killer's mouth!

But before Obi-Wan could do anything, the sea killer released them.

"What happened?" Obi-Wan asked.

They looked back. An even larger fish was chomping on the sea killer!

"Oyi!" Jar Jar said. "Sando aqua monster."

"I guess there's always a bigger fish," Obi-Wan said.

Qui-Gon nodded. "Very good, my young Padawan. You are beginning to see that all life forms serve a purpose."

"Mighty yesa," said Jar Jar. "Even when dey da main course!"

Obi-Wan steered the bongo deeper into the tunnel. But the sea killer had damaged the ship. Water was leaking into the cabin. Sparks flew from the controls. The lights flickered and then went out.

"We've lost power!" said Obi-Wan. He tinkered with the wiring.

The bongo drifted in total darkness.

"Weesa gonna die!" Jar Jar moaned.

"Stay calm," Qui-Gon said. "We're not in trouble yet."

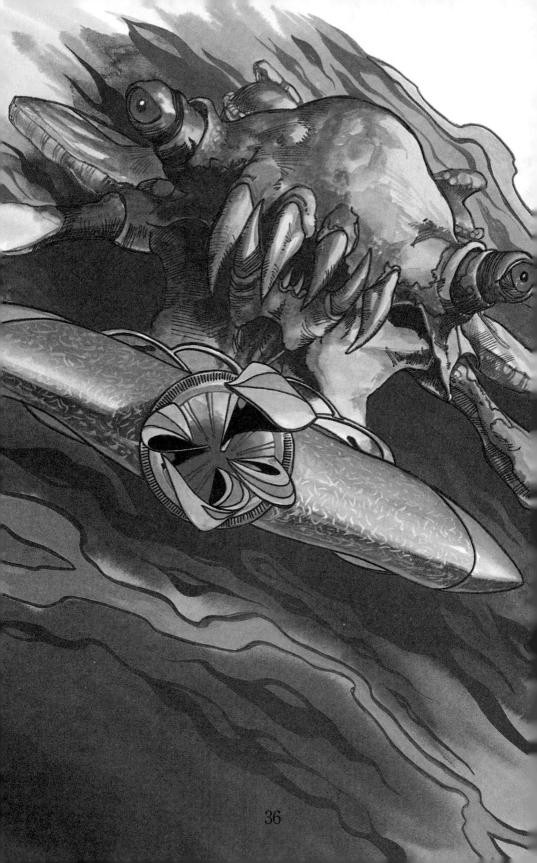

The lights popped back on.

"I got the power back," Obi-Wan said.

"Monster's back, too!" said Jar Jar.

In front of the bongo blinked a surprised colo claw fish.

Obi-Wan quickly spun the bongo around and headed back the way they had come. The claw fish saw its dinner escaping and chased after them.

Suddenly, Jar Jar jumped into Obi-Wan's lap.

"What are you doing?" Obi-Wan cried. "I can't see!"

The bongo swerved sharply from side to side because Jar Jar was holding Obi-Wan so tightly.

"Sando aqua monster!" cried Jar Jar, hiding his face in Obi-Wan's shirt.

Obi-Wan had forgotten about the aqua monster. Its teeth flashed in front of the cockpit and snapped shut just after the bongo passed. They'd just missed being eaten!

The colo claw fish wasn't so lucky. The Jedi watched as the aqua monster bit it in two.

Slowly, Jar Jar climbed back into his seat. "Phew!" he said. "Dat was a close one!"

Obi-Wan nodded. "Too close," he said. "But thanks for reminding me about the sando aqua monster."

Obi-Wan looked at Qui-Gon.

Qui-Gon nodded at him and smiled.

4
Theed

A short time later, Obi-Wan steered the bongo to the surface. They had made it safely through the dangerous core!

Jar Jar opened the hatch. In the distance they could see the sparkling towers of Theed.

"Weesa safe now," Jar Jar said.

But then they heard the sound of rushing water.

Obi-Wan and Jar Jar turned and looked behind them. They were drifting backward—toward a waterfall!

"Get this thing started!" Qui-Gon said.

Obi-Wan tried to restart the engine, but it wasn't working. The bongo was nearly at the edge of the waterfall!

Quickly, Qui-Gon pulled a cable from his belt and whipped it toward the shore. The cable snagged a railing—and held. The bongo stopped just in time!

"Hurry," Qui-Gon said. "We don't know how long it will hold."

Obi-Wan climbed out and pulled himself through the water toward the shore. Qui-Gon followed.

But Jar Jar didn't.

He sat in the bongo, shivering with fear!

"Come on, Jar Jar," Qui-Gon called.

Jar Jar shook his head. "No! Too scary!"

Obi-Wan was frustrated. "Jar Jar, get over here!" he shouted

"No, a mighty no!" Jar Jar replied. Then he looked over his shoulder. The bottom of the waterfall was hundreds of feet down. He sprang out of the bongo.

"Oie boie," he cried. "Meesa comin, meesa comin!"

On shore, Obi-Wan was helping
Qui-Gon out of the water when a clicking
noise echoed behind him. A battle droid
had its blaster pointed right at them!

"Drop your weapons," the droid said.

Just then, Jar Jar pulled himself onto shore, gasping for breath.

The battle droid turned its blaster on Jar Jar. "Halt!" it said.

Qui-Gon drew his lightsaber. With a single swift stroke, he cut the battle droid in half.

Obi-Wan looked at the droid, then back
at Jar Jar. He was slowly getting to his
feet.

Obi-Wan grinned. "Thanks, Jar Jar."

The young Jedi looked at Qui-Gon. "Maybe it wasn't such a bad idea to take him along, after all."

The older Jedi smiled and nodded. "You learn well, my young Padawan."

The three set off for the city of Theed. Surely their adventures together were not over!